Topic: Useful Tools   **Subtopic:** Things Around the House

Notes to Parents and Teachers:

At this level of reading, your child will rely less on the pattern of the words in the book and more on reading strategies to figure out the words in the story.

REMEMBER: PRAISE IS A GREAT MOTIVATOR!

Here are some praise points for beginning readers:

- You matched your finger to each word that you read!
- I like the way you used the picture to help you figure out that word.
- I noticed that you saw some sight words you knew how to read!

Book Ends for the Reader!

Here are some reminders before reading the text:

- Use picture clues to help figure out words.

- Get your mouth ready to say the first sound in a word and then stretch out the word by saying the sounds all the way through the word.

- Skip a word you do not know, and read the rest of a sentence to see what word would make sense in that sentence.

- Use sight words to help you figure out other words in the sentence.

Words to Know Before You Read

bottles

boxes

cans

moon

newspapers

rocket

space suits

wings

HOW DO WE GET
to the
MOON?

By Robert Rosen

Illustrated by Brett Curzon

Rourke
Educational Media
rourkeeducationalmedia.com

Barry and Terry are making a rocket.

GLUE

CRAFT

What can we use to make the body?

How about these old boxes?

They can be for the body.
I like it!

How do we get to the moon?

CRAFT

We need boosters!

How about these plastic bottles?

They can be for the boosters.
I like it!

How will our rocket fly?

We need wings!

How about these cans? We can tape them together.

They can be for the wings.
I like it!

How will we walk on the moon?

We need space suits!

GLUE

How about these old newspapers?

They can be for the space suits.
I like it!

Time to go to space.

3, 2, 1, BLAST OFF!

Book Ends for the Reader

I know...

1. What are Terry and Barry doing?

2. How are they making the body?

3. Why do they need boosters?

I think ...

1. Have you ever thought about going to the moon?

2. Have you ever made a rocket to go to the moon?

3. In the story, Terry and Barry used boxes, plastic bottles, cans and newspapers. Why do you think they used those materials?

Book Ends for the Reader

What happened in this book?

Look at each picture and talk about what happened in the story.

About the Author

Robert Rosen lives in South Korea with his wife, son and dog. He has taught kindergarten and elementary students since 2010. He likes to travel the world riding new roller coasters.

About the Illustrator

Born in Sydney Australia, Brett Curzon now lives in northern NSW Australia with his family, his wife, three kids, two dogs and one evil cat. Brett Curzon's whimsical art can be seen in children's books to drink bottles. If not working away, he can be found in the ocean, or at the very least only a few feet away.

Library of Congress PCN Data

How Do We Get to the Moon? / Robert Rosen

ISBN 978-1-68342-733-9 (hard cover)(alk. paper)
ISBN 978-1-68342-785-8 (soft cover)
ISBN 978-1-68342-837-4 (e-Book)
Library of Congress Control Number: 2017935449

Rourke Educational Media
Printed in the United States of America, North Mankato, Minnesota

© 2018 Rourke Educational Media

www.rourkeeducationalmedia.com

Edited by: Debra Ankiel
Art direction and layout by: Rhea Magaro-Wallace
Cover and interior Illustrations by: Brett Curzon